Contents

Ladybird books are widely available, but in case of
difficulty may be ordered by post or telephone from:

Ladybird Books – Cash Sales Department
Littlegate Road Paignton Devon TQ3 3BE
Telephone 0803 554761

A catalogue record for this book is available
from the British Library

Published by Ladybird Books Ltd Loughborough Leicestershire UK
Ladybird Books Inc Auburn Maine 04210 USA

Two
Minute
◆
Bunny
Tales

by Nicola Baxter

illustrated by Steve Smallman

The Rainbow Rabbits

"Who's got my SOCKS?" cried Mr Rabbit one morning. "Just wait until I find out which one of you naughty little bunnies has got them. Now then, Bayleaf, show me your FEET!"

But the little rabbit just giggled. "I'm not Bayleaf, Dad," he said innocently. "I'm Bluebell. And these aren't YOUR socks, they're Hazel's. And Hazel is wearing Scarlet's socks. And Scarlet is wearing Snowdrop's socks. And Rosebud isn't wearing any socks at all. And…"

"Stop!" cried Mr Rabbit. "You're making my ears spin." He peered closely at the little bunny in front of him. "Are you SURE you're not Bayleaf? No? Well never mind. The point is that everything is in a MUDDLE. No one knows who's wearing what, and I still haven't found my SOCKS! There's only one answer to a mess like this—we need a SYSTEM."

Mrs Rabbit sighed. She remembered her husband's PATENT IMPROVED CARROT COOKING SYSTEM—the steam had peeled off all the wallpaper—and as for

his WATER-SAVING EAR-WASHING SYSTEM—her ears had lost their wiggle for WEEKS!

Before long the floor was tail-deep in paper. "Don't stand on those charts!" cried Mr Rabbit, waving his crayons. "Now, everybody stand still and listen! My new system is based on COLOUR CO-ORDINATION! And," he added modestly, "it's brilliant! What do you think?"

"It's brilliant!" said Mrs Rabbit faintly.

And in a few days Mr Rabbit's system was in operation. Little Scarlet was dressed from paws to ears all in red. Primrose was all in yellow. You can guess what happened to Bayleaf, Snowdrop, Hazel, Bluebell and Rosebud!

At first the seven little bunnies rather liked looking different, but pretty soon they started to complain.

"I don't LIKE brown," said Hazel. "I want a tee-shirt like Bluebell's!"

"I'm never going to get dressed again if I have to wear horrible GREEN!" wailed Bayleaf.

Mrs Rabbit could hardly think straight with all the complaining; whereas Mr Rabbit insisted that, with a few minor adjustments, everything would be fine.

He set to work again
with his famous
crayons. But at the
end of the day he
accidentally left the
crayons in his shirt pocket
and then put the shirt in the washing
machine with all the children's clothes.

When Mrs Rabbit took the washing out of
the machine next morning, she laughed so
loud that the little rabbits came running.
"What's the matter, Mum?" they asked.

Mrs Rabbit choked and sniffled. "I don't want to hear one more word about... ho ho ho... your clothes," she giggled. "Your father has... hee hee hee... invented a new system called... ha ha ha... the ***IMPROVED*** COLOUR CO-ORDINATION SYSTEM – and we're ALL going to be using it!"

The little rabbits loved their multi-coloured clothes.

"It was time for – hh-hmm! – PHASE TWO of my System," said Mr Rabbit, looking aimlessly at the ceiling.

Another story tomorrow.

11

Slippy and the Skaters

There was once a bunny called Cowslip who was very clumsy. She bumped into furniture; she dropped her toast on the floor – jam side down – and she tripped over her own feet.

When Cowslip poured herself a drink, her mum would say, "Give that to me, Slippy. I'LL carry it into the dining room. We don't want MORE milk in the pot plants, do we?"

Cowslip didn't mean to be careless. It was just that she didn't think about what she was doing. And her mind was always on something else.

At playgroup the little bunnies ran round the room to music.

Hoppity, skippety, JUMP!
Hoppity, skippety, JUMP!
Hoppity, skippety, BUMP!

Yes, that was Cowslip. She'd noticed a spider high up on the ceiling and had forgotten to jump.

It seemed that hardly a day went by without Cowslip colliding into one of her friends or spilling her food – OR without someone telling her to concentrate and THINK about what she was doing.

One winter the water in the village pond froze so hard that it was safe to skate on. All the little bunnies, and some of the big ones as well, whizzed and swooped across the ice. Cowslip went along too, and started to put on her skates.

"Oh Slippy, PLEASE don't come on the ice!" shouted her brother. "You're sure to knock everyone over!"

"Perhaps you'd better just sit quietly on the bank and think, Slippy," advised her mum, who was practising her famous double-axel bunny-loop.

So Cowslip sat down on the bank and enjoyed watching her mum. She was a brilliant skater.

Soon the little bunny's mind moved on to other things. She noticed the way the ducks slithered and slipped on the ice, and wondered why they didn't wear skates; she noticed that old Bunny Hopkins was wearing odd socks and that his jacket didn't quite fit; she noticed that the ice was melting in the middle of the pond...

WHAT? "STOP!" cried Cowslip. "The ice is melting!"

In only a minute or two all the skaters were safely off the ice. Now they could see the growing hole in the middle, too.

"Well done, Slippy," said her mum. "You were the only one thinking about the really important things. My double-axel bunny-loop and your brothers and sisters might never have been seen again!"

Another story tomorrow.

17

The Dancing Bunny

Do you know young Hoppy
Who can never keep still?
If you haven't seen him,
Then you certainly will.

He jigs in the sunshine,
He hops in the drizzle,
He zooms out of the house,
With a double-toed twizzle.

From breakfast to supper
He dances and jiggles,
He waggles and waltzes,
He prances and wiggles.

And when sleepy Hoppy
Is tucked up in bed,
He's dancing the foxtrot
Inside his own head!

Turn over for another bunny rhyme.

Visiting Wizard Whee

Five little bunnies
Knocking on the wizard's door;
One was rather nervous,
So then there were four!

Four little bunnies
Said hello to Wizard Whee;
One went home with hiccups
So then there were three!

Three little bunnies
Found some magic spells to do;
But they muddled up the words,
So then there were two!

Two little bunnies
Having lots of wizard fun;
One found a magic hat,
So then there was one!

One little bunny
Wished his friends were back again;
The naughty wizard said a spell,
And then there were ten!

Turn over for another bunny rhyme.

21

Mrs Bunny Had Twins...

What wonderful news!
But what names would she choose?
So many relatives
Had their own views.

Said old uncle Boris,
"Have you thought of Horace?
And Doris? Or Morris?
Or Norris? Or... BORIS?"

Smiled grandmother Connie,
"Dear, what about Ronnie?
And Bonnie? Or Jonnie?
Or Lonnie? Or... CONNIE?"

Cried young cousin Harry,
"But what about Barry?
And Carrie? Or Larry?
Or Gary? Or... HARRY?"

Laughed poor Mrs Bunny,
"Here's Sonny. Here's Honey.
For names don't sound funny,
When they rhyme with... BUNNY!"

Another story tomorrow.

23

The Trouble With Babies

One day Timmy's mum sat him on her knee. "Timmy," she said, "soon you are going to have some little brothers and sisters to play with. Won't that be nice?"

Timmy was very excited. He was tired of playing all by himself and he could hardly wait for the new bunnies to be born. He tidied up his toy box and started to think of good games he could play with his brothers and sisters. He lined up all his cars and his big yellow tractor under the table. "This can be Timmy's Garage," he thought. "The little bunnies can drive my cars and I will be Chief Mechanic."

"Come and see your new brothers and sisters!" said Timmy's dad a few days later. Mum was sitting up in bed holding four little bundles. Timmy tip-toed forward.

"But they're tiny!" he squeaked in surprise. They certainly didn't look big enough to drive his big yellow tractor.

"They'll grow very fast," laughed Mum.

But things didn't get better next day or the day after that. The babies didn't grow very fast at all. They seemed to be asleep nearly all the time – and they wouldn't even open their eyes!

A few weeks later the little bunnies started to smile and gurgle. Timmy waited until his mum was out of the room.

"It's all right," he whispered to his brothers and sisters. "She's not here. You can stop pretending now and talk to me."

But the little bunnies just smiled and gurgled again.

"Come and see my garage," said Timmy. But the little bunnies didn't seem at all interested.

Mum found Timmy looking sad. "My new brothers and sisters don't like me," he said. "They won't talk to me and they don't want to share my toys."

"But Timmy," said his mum, "that's because they're only a few weeks old, and you are a BIG bunny now. They have a lot to learn, and YOU can help me to teach them to do all the things that you can do."

So Timmy put away his cars and his big yellow tractor. "Little bunnies are not ready to play with big toys yet. They have a lot to learn," he announced. Then he piled some cushions and his picture books under the table. "This is Timmy's School," he said. "And I am the Baby Bunny Teacher!"

Another story tomorrow.

Everard's Ears

Once there was a bunny called Everard who had extra-large ears.

"Everard, your ears are ENORMOUS!" laughed his friends Basil and Beech.

Everard's ears started drooping, and he looked very unhappy.

"It's all right! You just haven't grown into your ears yet, son," said Everard's dad. "And, who knows, one day you may find they come in useful."

But Everard couldn't think of a single reason why big ears would ever be of any use at all. And it seemed his friends would NEVER stop teasing him.

"Shouldn't you put flashing lights on your ears to warn low-flying aircraft?" asked Basil.

"No wonder there's a hole in the ozone layer," giggled Beech.

Everard's ears drooped down even further.

"Ears up, son," said Evcrard's dad. "Any rabbit can have ORDINARY ears, but you're my EXTRAORDINARY Everard. And don't you forget it!"

Now there was a big cabbage field
nearby, and whenever there was washing
up or bedroom tidying to be done,
Everard, Basil and Beech would hop off
into the field to hide. They would sit
among the huge cabbages, nibble leaves
or play games – and wait until they
thought it was safe to go home.

One afternoon in the cabbage field, Beech started laughing. "Everard!" he giggled, holding two big cabbage leaves above his head. "What do these remind you of?"

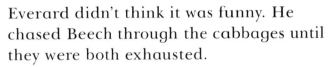

Everard didn't think it was funny. He chased Beech through the cabbages until they were both exhausted.

"Stop!" puffed Basil, trailing along behind. "Where are we?" The cabbages had grown so high that the bunnies couldn't see which way to go.

After hours of running in all directions, the three bunnies were near to tears. "We'll be here for EVER!" said Beech. "I'm sorry, Everard, it's all my fault!"

The frightened little bunnies flopped down among the cabbages. "No one will ever find us," sobbed Basil.

"But, if we ever do get out, we promise never to make fun of you-know-what again, Everard!"

A few minutes later they heard a cheery voice nearby. "Come on, boys," said Everard's dad. "I'll show you the way home. It's lucky I reached you before it got dark."

"How ever did you find us?" asked Beech, as they all tramped home together.

Everard's dad looked down at his son's ears waving above the cabbages. He gave Everard a big wink. "Let's just say I had EXTRAORDINARY good luck," he said.

Another story tomorrow.

35

The Princess Bunny

One night Holly's babysitter read her a bedtime story about a princess who was kept prisoner by a dragon. A brave prince rescued the princess and she lived happily ever after.

"I'd like to be a princess," said Holly to her little brother Ben. "But I'd quite like to do the brave rescuing too."

"Huh," said Ben sleepily. "I'd rather be a dragon."

A few days later, as Holly took a short-cut across the farmyard, she nearly hopped into a wire fence.

"That wasn't here before," she muttered. She was just about to go on when she saw a beautiful bunny inside the fence.

"She must be a princess!" gasped Holly. The new rabbit had long white fur and a tiny pink nose.

Holly didn't think twice. "Don't worry," she cried. "It's Holly here. I'll rescue you!" She found a little gate in the fence, pushed open the bolt, and hopped inside.

"Delighted to meet you. I'm Florabell," said the bunny. "What...?"

"Just follow me," said Holly. "There's no time to lose!"

So the princess bunny hopped into the farmyard. "I'm not sure..." she said.

"COME ON!" cried Holly. "Can't you hop any faster?" And she scampered into the next-door meadow.

"I'm not used to hopping over FIELDS," complained Florabell. And she flopped down and wouldn't go any further.

"It's very kind of you to visit," she said, "although I don't really like hopping games. Anyway I think I must get back now. It's time for my dinner."

"But I'm rescuing you!" wailed Holly.

"Well, it's been very nice to meet you," said Florabell. "But I've got a very cosy house of my own and a little boy brings me lovely things to eat. He'd be so sad if I got lost. You must drop round for another delightful chat some time. Goodbye!" And Florabell hopped cheerfully home.

Next time the babysitter came she asked if Holly and Ben would like the story about the Princess again.

"No thank you," said Holly. "We'd like a story with lots of dragons and no princesses AT ALL!"

Turn over for another bunny rhyme.

41

Belinda's Bedtime

When it was time to go to bed,
Belinda Bunny always said,
"I'm just not ready yet to go.
I'm not a baby now you know!"

One night her mother counted ten
And sat down in her chair again.
"This fuss is more than I can take.
All right, Belinda, stay awake!"

This was a very big surprise!
Belinda yawned and rubbed her eyes.
Now that her mum had let her stay,
She really felt too tired to play.

A minute passed – it seemed like ten!
Belinda's voice was heard again.
"I think it's time to go to bed,
I'm only little still," she said.

The end.

43